Acting Edition

The Best School Year Ever

by Jahnna Beecham
& Malcolm Hillgartner

Based on the book
The Best School Year Ever
by Barbara Robinson

FOR PRODUCTION INQUIRIES

UNITED STATES AND CANADA
info@concordtheatricals.com
1-866-979-0447

UNITED KINGDOM AND EUROPE
licensing@concordtheatricals.co.uk
020-7054-7298

Each title is subject to availability from Concord Theatricals Corp., depending upon country of performance. Please be aware that *THE BEST SCHOOL YEAR EVER* may not be licensed by Concord Theatricals Corp. in your territory. Professional and amateur producers should contact the nearest Concord Theatricals Corp. office or licensing partner to verify availability.

No one shall make any changes in this title(s) for the purpose of production. No part of this book may be reproduced, stored in a retrieval system, scanned, uploaded, or transmitted in any form, by any means, now known or yet to be invented, including mechanical, electronic, digital, photocopying, recording, videotaping, or otherwise, without the prior written permission of the publisher. No one shall share this title(s), or any part of this title(s), through any social media or file hosting websites.

For all inquiries regarding motion picture, television, online/digital and other media rights, please contact Concord Theatricals Corp.

MUSIC AND THIRD-PARTY MATERIALS USE NOTE

Licensees are solely responsible for obtaining formal written permission from copyright owners to use copyrighted music and/or other copyrighted third-party materials (e.g. artworks, logos) in the performance of this play and are strongly cautioned to do so. If no such permission is obtained by the licensee, then the licensee must use only original music and materials that the licensee owns and controls. Licensees are solely responsible and liable for clearances of all third-party copyrighted materials, including without limitation music, and shall indemnify the copyright owners of the play(s) and their licensing agent, Concord Theatricals Corp., against any costs, expenses, losses and liabilities arising from the use of such copyrighted third-party materials by licensees. For music, please contact the appropriate music licensing authority in your territory for the rights to any incidental music.

IMPORTANT BILLING AND CREDIT REQUIREMENTS

If you have obtained performance rights to this title, please refer to your licensing agreement for important billing and credit requirements.

The world premiere of *THE BEST SCHOOL YEAR EVER was* produced by Nashville Children's Theatre in Nashville, TN, on September 7th, 2024. The performance was directed by Ernie Nolan, with sets and lighting by Scott Leathers, costumes by Billy Ditty, and sound design by Marsalis Turner. The Production Stage Manager was Will Farris. The cast was as follows:

BETH BRADLEY . . . . Joy Pointe

CHARLIE BRADLEY . . . . Gerold Oliver

MRS. BRADLEY/MISS KEMP/MRS. MCCLUSKY/
    NURSE GREENBLATT . . . . Tamiko Robison Steele

IMOGENE HERDMAN . . . . Sejal Mehta

LEROY HERDMAN/EUGENE PRESTON . . . . Brian Jones

GLADYS HERDMAN/MISS NEWMAN . . . . Alisa Osborne

ALICE WENDLEKEN/MRS. WENDLEKEN . . . . Erika Haines

BOOMER MALONE . . . . Will Henke

LOUELLA MCCLUSKY . . . . Natalie Rankin

THE BEST SCHOOL YEAR EVER received a developmental reading with Nashville Children's Theatre on July 19th 2024.

CHARACTERS

BETH BRADLEY – Earnest narrator of this story who sees the irony in a lot of what's happening. This fifth grader tries her best to be straightforward and kind to everyone, but the Herdmans make it difficult sometimes.

CHARLIE BRADLEY – The traditional kid brother who is a bit goofy and a little intimidated by older kids, especially the Herdmans.

MRS. BRADLEY – Unflappable, witty mom.

IMOGENE HERDMAN – (Pronounced "IM-UH-JEEN") Bossy fifth grader, leader of the Herdmans. She's very matter-of-fact and has her own logic.

LEROY HERDMAN – Imogene's sly fox of a brother in third grade. He enjoys teasing other kids. He rarely smiles.

GLADYS HERDMAN – Small and feisty first grader. She bites. She's dead serious.

ALICE WENDLEKEN – This prim and proper fifth grader is a know-it-all and can be a tattletale if rules aren't followed.

BOOMER MALONE – This likeable fifth grader loves sports, is friendly to everyone and is unaware that several girls have crushes on him.

EUGENE PRESTON – (played by **LEROY**) – Painfully shy third grader who mumbles and has a hard time looking people in the eye.

LOUELLA MCCLUSKY – Beth's best friend in fifth grade who over-reacts to most situations. She can be really mad. Or really in love. Or really silly.

MISS KEMP – (Beth's teacher, played by **MRS. BRADLEY**) – She wears glasses with bold frames and is an enthusiastic teacher who loves her students.

MRS. MCCLUSKY – (played by **GLADYS**) – A harried mom. We meet her at the hair salon in foils and a brightly-colored cape.

MRS. WENDLEKEN – (played by **ALICE**) – A self-righteous gossip who is not above bending the rules if it will benefit her perfect daughter Alice.

NURSE GREENBLATT – (played by **MRS. BRADLEY**) – She is an unflappable ex-army nurse. Nothing surprises her anymore.

MISS NEWMAN – (played by **GLADYS**) – This very earnest, easily startled teacher wears wire-rimmed glasses and has frazzled-looking hair. She has lost the battle with the Herdmans and is a nervous wreck.

BABY HOWARD MCCLUSKY – a doll or puppet in a baby carriage, then in a stroller. We see the tattooed top of his head over the curtain.

RECORDED VOICES

PRINCIPAL CRABTREE – Over the microphone, he is an enthusiastic leader of the school who tries to make his daily announcements entertaining, contrasting with his impatience off-microphone with everyone who works with him.

RALPH HERDMAN – Sixth grader. He's the enforcer in the family.

CLAUDE HERDMAN – Fourth grader.

OLLIE HERDMAN – Second grader.

VICE PRINCIPAL DURWOOD PELFREY – Kind of a dorky assistant.

SCHOOL SECRETARY MRS. PROCTOR – Prim and proper.

VOLUNTEER MOM – Traffic cop at the Hug-n-Go.

MRS. WENDLEKEN – Stuck in the teachers' lounge.

KIDS – Chanting "Hammerhead! Hammerhead!" during the talent show.

SETTING

The play takes place in several locations:

The Bradley house:

> Beth and Charlie's shared room.
>
> The Bradley kitchen with phone/Mrs. Wendleken's kitchen with phone.
>
> Mrs. Bradley's car driving to and from Woodrow Wilson Elementary School.

Woodrow Wilson Elementary School:

> The hallway lined with lockers.
>
> Miss Kemp's fifth grade classroom with rolling blackboard.
>
> The lunchroom with a table.
>
> The door to the mysterious teachers' lounge.
>
> The door to the nurse's office.
>
> The Hug-n-Go drop off in front of the school.
>
> The playground.
>
> Backstage/onstage at the school auditorium.

Neighborhood shopping area.

> The storefront of mom-and-pop grocery with beauty salon attached.
>
> A vacant lot with clothesline.

TIME

This play, like the book it is based on, has the feel of an earlier time around the 1960s or early 1970s, when unsupervised kids freely rode their bikes around neighborhoods and phones were attached by long cords to walls. Most moms stayed home to care for their families while the dads worked. Babysitters were paid fifty cents an hour. And the worst thing a kid could do would be to shoplift a candy bar or accidentally set fire to someone's tool shed.

AUTHOR'S NOTES

The set can be a series of panels that roll on and off. They can have different set elements on both sides. Benches, chairs and tables can be configured to create other elements.

The school hallway can be defined by two rolling panels of lockers with doors that open. One panel can be turned to have Miss Kemp's classroom blackboard on the other side. The other panel can be Beth and Charlie's bedroom wall.

Mrs. Bradley's car could be two benches to indicate the front and back seat. Or a two-step stair unit. Mrs. Bradley can either hold a steering wheel, or mime one.

The benches or step unit can become the seats at the lunchroom or used for the classroom or on the playground.

Desks can also be on wheels and be put together to be a lunch table. Or they can be several step units.

Door to the teachers' lounge could have a door to the nurse's office on the other side.

Ranger Bear is a freestanding cutout on wheels.

SOUND EFFECTS

Clock chimes
School bell
Sounds of kids talking; locker doors slamming
Fire alarm
Kids cheering
Kids' voices: "Go, Imogene! Woohoo!"
Fire truck siren
Loud whistle
Car horn
Car engine driving
Car brakes
Carnival music
Baby cries
Mixed responses from students
Holiday music on car radio
"Jingle Bells"
Holiday instrumental
Last bars of Alice's "Flying Fingers" piano music (just fast piano)
"Waltz Of The Flowers" from *The Nutcracker Suite*
Loud applause
Kids cheering
Knocking
Jump rope chant of girls on the playground
Loud knocking and pounding on teachers' lounge door

Scene One
Bradley House, Kids' Bedroom – September

(**BETH** *is in one twin bed, having a nightmare, calling out.* **CHARLIE** *is in the other.*)

(*Sound effects: Clock chimes three a.m.*)

BETH. Mom! Mommmmmm! Ouch, that hurt! Stop it! Help! Mom!

CHARLIE. Mom! Don't help Beth – help me! Stay back!

(**MRS. BRADLEY** *appears at the door in her robe. She has curlers in her hair.*)

MRS. BRADLEY. What is going on in here? Charlie? Beth? Why is everyone shouting?

BETH. I had a nightmare.

CHARLIE. So did I!

BETH. It was the first day of school, and I had to take a note to the teachers' lounge, and Imogene and Gladys Herdman were there.

MRS. BRADLEY. That's impossible! Kids are never ever allowed in the teachers' lounge. Especially not the Herdmans.

BETH. Well, they were there, and Gladys was biting me. And Imogene stole my lunch and ate everything but the carrots.

CHARLIE. And I couldn't get into my locker 'cause I forgot the combination.

1

MRS. BRADLEY. Charlie, you know it by heart.

CHARLIE. Then I discovered that all six Herdmans were in my class.

MRS. BRADLEY. That could never happen. They are all different ages.

BETH. The teachers could have held them back.

MRS. BRADLEY. No teacher wants to spend two years with the same Herdman.

BETH. You're right! That would be insane.

(To audience.) The Herdmans are the worst kids in the history of the world! They tell lies and smoke smelly cigars, set fire to stuff, stay away from school whenever they want. And every September I pray that maybe this year the Herdmans will be gone. But every year, there they are on the first day of school, up to their old tricks.

*(While **BETH** talks to the audience, **MRS. BRADLEY** is shuffling around picking up their room.)*

MRS. BRADLEY. Charlie, why are you sleeping in your clothes?

CHARLIE. I want to get to school early so I can sit in the front row and not have to sit next to Leroy Herdman. He's mean.

BETH. That's a good idea. I should get dressed. We can go early and I won't have to sit next to Imogene.

(To audience.) She's meaner than Leroy.

MRS. BRADLEY. Whoa, whoa, whoa! It's three in the morning and I'm the one who will be driving you to school and I'm *not* getting up or getting dressed.

*(**CHARLIE** is out of bed, stuffing items into his backpack.)*

CHARLIE. Beth, I'll give you two candy bars for extra pencils.

MRS. BRADLEY. Why do you have candy bars?

BETH & CHARLIE. To trade.

CHARLIE. When they try to steal our lunches. I always offer a candy bar instead.

MRS. BRADLEY. That works?

BETH. Of course. Who wouldn't want a candy bar?

(Hands **CHARLIE** *some pencils.)*

Here's four.

CHARLIE. Thanks. Leroy is a big pencil thief.

MRS. BRADLEY. *(Looking over* **CHARLIE***'s shoulder into his pack.)* Is that bug spray?

CHARLIE. Yeah. In case Ralph Herdman releases spiders in the lunchroom like he did last year.

BETH. Don't forget the Band-Aids and antibiotic cream.

MRS. BRADLEY. What for?

BETH. Gladys. She bites.

*(***CHARLIE*** stuffs a catcher's mask in his bag or puts it on.)*

CHARLIE. And just in case there's punching and kicking...

BETH. Good point!

(She grabs a bike helmet and puts it on.)

MRS. BRADLEY. You two are being silly. Go back to bed. The first day of school should be fun.

CHARLIE. Fun?

BETH. *(To audience.)* It'll be a nightmare.

(**BETH** *and* **CHARLIE** *fall back in bed, clutching their backpacks, and* **MRS. BRADLEY** *flicks off the light.*)

(*Sound effects: School bell.*)

Scene Two
Woodrow Wilson Elementary Hallway

(First day of school. The crowded hallway lined with lockers decorated with "Welcome Back!" signs.)

(Sound effects: Sounds of kids talking; locker doors slamming.)

(Kids carry books, wear backpacks, and open locker doors. **LOUELLA**, **ALICE**, *and* **BOOMER** *are first to appear. Behind them with backs turne, are* **LEROY**, **GLADYS** *and* **IMOGENE**.*)*

[PA ANNOUNCEMENT]

PRINCIPAL. *(Voice-over.)* Welcome, students, to Woodrow Wilson Elementary. This school year should be better than ever. Find your lockers. If you can't remember your combination, we have them here in the office.

*(**LOUELLA** runs up to **ALICE**.)*

LOUELLA. Alice! I love your dress!

ALICE. Thank you, Louella. My mother got it in the city.

*(**BOOMER** enters.)*

LOUELLA. *(Whispers excitedly to **ALICE**.)* Look! It's Boomer!

ALICE & LOUELLA. Hi, Boomer!

*(**BOOMER** acknowledges both **GIRLS** as he heads for his locker.)*

BOOMER. Oh, hey!

*(**LOUELLA** turns to **ALICE** with a smile so big it looks like she's snarling.)*

LOUELLA. Notice anything different about me?

ALICE. Your hair?

LOUELLA. No.

ALICE. Your sweater?

LOUELLA. No.

ALICE. I give up.

LOUELLA. I got my braces off!

ALICE. *(Polite.)* Oh.

> (**CHARLIE** *enters trying different lockers, confused.)*

LOUELLA. Charlie, where's Beth?

CHARLIE. Uh, she's coming.

> (**BETH** *enters and calls.)*

BETH. Louella!

LOUELLA. There you are!

BETH. Our locker is over here.

> *(The* **HERDMANS** *appear, striking a menacing pose.)*

IMOGENE. Hey everybody!

LEROY, IMOGENE & GLADYS. We're back!

> *(The rest of the* **KIDS** *freeze, with panicked looks.)*

BETH, CHARLIE, LOUELLA, BOOMER & ALICE. Oh, no!

BETH. *(To audience.)* The Herdmans.

BOOMER. Guys! Hide your lunch.

*(The **KIDS** reach for their lunches, trying to hide them in their lockers as the **HERDMANS** move past the lockers trying to grab them.)*

*(**GLADYS** grabs **CHARLIE**'s bag lunch.)*

GLADYS. Tuna? Yuck!

*(**LEROY** grabs bag from **GLADYS**.)*

LEROY. I like tuna!

*(**IMOGENE** is pulling a wagon filled with stolen goods. She goes to **ALICE**.)*

IMOGENE. Fork it over!

*(**ALICE** hands over her fancy lunchbox.)*

ALICE. *(Mumbling.)* Not fair.

*(**GLADYS** grabs **BOOMER**'s lunch bag.)*

GLADYS. Egg salad? P-U!

*(**BOOMER MALONE**, baseball cap on his head, smoothly takes the egg salad lunch from **GLADYS** and tosses it in his locker, the walls of which are covered with sports posters.)*

BOOMER. All right! A Herdman-proof sandwich. Score, Mom!

*(**LOUELLA** holds up her lunchbox to **BETH**.)*

LOUELLA. I'm so happy. I can finally eat peanut butter and jelly again.

*(**GLADYS** snatches **LOUELLA**'s lunchbox.)*

GLADYS. Thanks, I'll take that.

LOUELLA. Gladys, give that back!

GLADYS. Come and get it!

IMOGENE. Outta my way!

> (**IMOGENE** *takes the lunchbox from* **GLADYS.**)

Thanks, Gladys!

GLADYS. Imogene, that's mine!

IMOGENE. Not anymore.

IMOGENE. *(To* **LEROY** *who is holding a Twinkie.*)* I see Twinkies! Give it here.

> (**IMOGENE** *tries to grab the Twinkie from* **LEROY.**)

> (**LEROY** *takes a huge bite of Twinkie.*)

LEROY. Now you see it, now you don't.

> (**CHARLIE** *runs up to* **BETH.**)

CHARLIE. Beth, I can't remember which locker is mine.

BETH. You're between Boomer Malone and Leroy Herdman.

LEROY. That's my name, don't wear it out.

CHARLIE. *(Whispers to* **BETH.**) Why do I always have to be next to Leroy?

BETH. Well, at least it isn't Ralph.

> (**CHARLIE** *moves to open his locker, trying to stay away from* **LEROY.**)

BOOMER. Where *is* Ralph?

LEROY. Don't look at me.

---

*A license to produce *The Best School Year Ever* does not include a license to publicly display any branded logos or trademarked images. Licensees must acquire rights for any logos and/or images or create their own.

ALICE. In the principal's office. He and Claude were caught letting the air out of kids' bike tires.

LOUELLA. On the first day of school?

ALICE. It's a good thing I told the principal.

BETH. *(To audience.)* See? The Herdmans are just as bad as last year.

LOUELLA. Wait a minute. There's Gladys, Leroy and Imogene. Where's Ollie?

> *(All look around nervously to make sure Ollie's not sneaking up on them to steal pencils or lunch.)*

BETH. *(To* **LOUELLA.***)* Probably with Ralph and Claude in the principal's office.

> *(As* **IMOGENE** *passes by,* **BOOMER** *notices his baseball glove in her loot wagon.)*

BOOMER. Hey, Imogene. That's my baseball mitt!

IMOGENE. Finders keepers.

BOOMER. But it's brand new...

BETH. *(To audience.)* What did I tell you? Imogene just takes things and doesn't care if anyone sees her!

> *(Sound effects: School bell.)*

[PA ANNOUNCEMENT]

PRINCIPAL. *(Voice-over.)* Attention, students, go to your classrooms. Today is a big day and teachers have a lot to cover. Go to your classrooms now.

> *(***KIDS** *close lockers, scoop up books, head to their classrooms.)*

BETH. *(To* **LOUELLA.***)* Come on. I want to get a seat in the front row.

LOUELLA. Beth? Notice anything different about me?

BETH. Yes. But I'm not sure what.

LOUELLA. It's my teeth. See?

BETH. Did you have them whitened?

LOUELLA. *(Frustrated.)* No! I got my braces off and not one person has noticed!

BETH. Sorry, Louella. They just look so shiny and white. Now hurry!

(They run off.)

*(**CHARLIE** struggles with his "safety equipment" and goes the wrong way.)*

CHARLIE. Oh, no. Where's my classroom?

*(**LEROY** leans against his locker, still finishing another kid's lunch.)*

LEROY. Not that way. That leads to the teachers' lounge. And you know what happens in there.

CHARLIE. No, what?

LEROY. *(Smiles smugly.)* That's for me to know and you to find out.

*(**LEROY** points at **CHARLIE**'s chest, **CHARLIE** looks down and **LEROY** flips his chin up.)*

Fooled ya!

*(**LEROY** grabs something from **CHARLIE** like a hat or a catcher's mask and runs off.)*

CHARLIE. *(Follows **LEROY**.)* Leroy, give that back!

(Sound effects: School bell.)

Scene Three
Miss Kemp's Classroom

(**MISS KEMP** *is writing on a rolling blackboard that says "Miss Kemp" and "Welcome, 5th Grade!"* **ALICE** *and* **BOOMER** *are at their desks.* **BETH** *and* **LOUELLA** *take their seats.* **IMOGENE**, *still pulling her wagon, knocks* **LOUELLA** *out of her seat and sits in it.)*

IMOGENE. Move it!

LOUELLA. *(Voice peters out as she looks for a different seat.)* That was my seat.

IMOGENE. Wait a minute. Did you get your braces off?

LOUELLA. You noticed!

IMOGENE. Of course. No more metal mouth.

(**IMOGENE** *shoves a round oatmeal box in* **BETH**'s *face and shakes it. There's a lot of thumping and squeaking inside.)*

Hey, Beth Bradley! You want to buy a science project?

BETH. *(Flinching away from the box.)* Does it explode or catch fire?

IMOGENE. Not this year.

BETH. Well, I don't know if we're even going to do a science project.

IMOGENE. Then what am I going to do with these mice?

(**ALICE** *leaps to her feet in horror.)*

ALICE. Mice!

BETH. I don't know. Let them go –

ALICE. *(Squeals.)* Miss Kemp!

BETH. – outside?

IMOGENE. Not till I know for sure.

> (**MISS KEMP** *puts the chalk down, turns around, addresses her class.*)

MISS KEMP. Welcome, Fifth Grade. It's so good to see your shiny faces back in school. There's a lot for us to do today but first, I'm excited to tell you about Woodrow Wilson Elementary's big theme for this year. It's called "Kids Really Care." Can you repeat that?

ALL KIDS. Kids Really Care!

MISS KEMP. Great! Our school will be doing a lot of projects that show how much you kids really care about this community and each other. But the biggest project is you are each going to write a Compliments for Classmates journal.

> (*The* **CLASS** *breaks into bewildered muttering:* "Compliments?" "What for?" "A whole journal?" "Do we have to?")

> (**BOOMER** *raises his hand.*)

BOOMER. Miss Kemp?

Well, I

MISS KEMP. Yes, Boomer.

BOOMER. I don't get it.

MISS KEMP. You will each get to know your classmates and write a page worth of compliments for every person in this class.

LOUELLA. That's a lot of compliments.

MISS KEMP. Don't worry, Louella. You have all year to work on it.

BOOMER. It's going to take a whole year?

MISS KEMP. Yes. This is a very big project. As big as the science fair last year. It's half of your citizenship grade!

ALL KIDS. Half?

MISS KEMP. And I'll give you extra points for including other kids in the school.

(**IMOGENE** *nudges* **BETH** *with the mouse box.*)

IMOGENE. Beth Bradley. What's a compliment?

BETH. It's when you say something nice about somebody.

IMOGENE. Then I don't like compliments.

(Lifts lid and peeks in her box.)

Mice are much better.

(While **BETH** *talks,* **MISS KEMP** *passes out the journals.* **ALICE** *receives her journal first.)*

BETH. *(To audience.)* For once in my life, I had to agree with Imogene. I can say nice things about most people, but there are a few kids that make it really hard.

ALICE. *(Smugly pats her own hair.)* Miss Kemp, would shiny *and* beautiful hair count as one compliment, or two?

BETH. *(Lowers her voice.)* I mean, Alice Wendleken can be pretty stuck-up and kind of a tattle-tale.

MISS KEMP. Those *could* be considered compliments, Alice, but we're not talking about outward looks. I want to know what you think is good and interesting and special *inside* your classmates.

(**IMOGENE** *makes sure she gets the next journal, jumping out of her seat.*)

IMOGENE. I'll take that one! It's the best.

MISS KEMP. Okay...

BETH. And Imogene is a big pain. She's got a box full of smelly mice in that wagon and –

(Looks at wagon.)

– a lot of other people's belongings. See? That's Patty Hume's purple hairbrush and Elmer's Spider-Man pencil box.* It's all sitting right there in plain sight. But if you even think about trying to get it back, she'll make you regret it for the rest of your life.

MISS KEMP. Okay, class. These are your journals for the year. Take good care of them. You can decorate the covers and fill them with compliments about your classmates.

IMOGENE. This is going to be hard.

       (BETH *looks at audience; others glare at* **IMOGENE.***)*

ALL KIDS. *Really* hard.

       (Sound effects: Fire alarm.)

       (KIDS *panic.)*

MISS KEMP. What's that?

BOOMER. The fire alarm!

ALICE & LOUELLA. Fire?

BETH. Where?

MISS KEMP. So soon? It's only the first day of school!

       (Sound effects: Kids can be heard cheering in other classrooms.)

---

* A license to produce *The Best School Year Ever* does not include a license to publicly display any branded logos or trademarked images. Licensees must acquire rights for any logos and/or images or create their own.

LOUELLA. What are we supposed to do?

IMOGENE. Break a window!

MISS KEMP. No!

BOOMER. Run!

MISS KEMP. No!

ALICE. Hide under the desk!

BETH. That's for tornadoes.

BOOMER. Stop, drop and roll!

MISS KEMP. No!

>*(Blows whistle.)*

On your feet, class. And stay calm. I'm sure it's just a drill.

BETH. Do you think some kid pulled the fire alarm?

IMOGENE. My brother Ollie.

BOOMER. Ollie? He's a second grader.

IMOGENE. Ralph bet Ollie a Snickers bar that he wouldn't pull the alarm. So Ollie wins!

MISS KEMP. Let's form a single line. Follow –

>*(**IMOGENE** runs to be first.)*

IMOGENE. Me!

MISS KEMP. *(Dismayed.)* Oooooooh-kay. Okay. Follow Imogene. Stay right behind her and in your line.

ALL KIDS. Yes, Miss Kemp.

IMOGENE. *(Marching in place.)* Hup! Two-three-four!

>*(The **CLASS** imitates **IMOGENE**, chanting, "Hup! Two-three-four.")*

MISS KEMP. *(Gathers purse and whistle.)* Walk to the front lawn and wait for the all-clear. Do not leave the school grounds.

BOOMER. That's what Ralph Herdman did last year.

ALICE. He led his entire class down to the basement and right out the back door –

LOUELLA. – and then straight to Johnson's Candy Store.

MISS KEMP. When you hear my whistle, everybody freeze. Got it?

ALL KIDS. Yes, Miss Kemp.

> *(As the **CLASS** marches out of classroom, **IMOGENE** barks out instructions.)*

IMOGENE. On your marks –

MISS KEMP. *(From the back of the line but still onstage.)* Slow down!

IMOGENE. *(Offstage.)* Get set –

MISS KEMP. I mean it, Imogene!

IMOGENE. Go!!

> *(**IMOGENE** takes off like the start of a race, with the whole **CLASS** behind her.)*

> *(Sound effects: Other kids' voices: "Go, Imogene! Woohoo!")*

> *(**MISS KEMP** blows whistle and runs offstage. The classroom transitions to the hallway.)*

Scene Four
The Hallway

(**IMOGENE** *and* **CLASS** *come running back across the stage the other way, followed by* **MISS KEMP**, *blowing the whistle. They run offstage with* **LEROY** *and* **CHARLIE** *joining their group.*)

MISS KEMP. Stop! (*Whistle.*) Children, stop! (*Whistle.*) Do you hear me?

[PA ANNOUNCEMENT]

PRINCIPAL. (*Voice-over.*) False alarm! There is no fire. No fire! Please return to your classrooms!

(*There's a kerfuffle heard in the background, as though someone's trying to grab the mic. It's* **RALPH** *and* **CLAUDE HERDMAN.**)

RALPH. (*Voice-over.*) Way to go, Ollie!

CLAUDE. (*Voice-over.*) Ralph owes you a Snickers!

(*Another* **VOICE** *is heard shouting.*)

VICE PRINCIPAL. (*Voice-over.*) It's a stampede! They're heading for the candy store!

RALPH & CLAUDE. (*Voice-over.*) Woohoo! Run, Ollie, run!

PRINCIPAL. (*Voice-over.*) Stop them, Derwood! Stop those kids!

(*Sound effects: Fire truck siren.*)

(**BETH** *returns with her Compliments for Classmates journal and backpack.*)

BETH. (*To audience.*) So that was just the first day of school with the Herdmans. For the rest of September, they each took turns pulling the fire alarm until Mr. Crabtree, the principal, finally taped over the alarm in the hallway.

PRINCIPAL. *(Voice-over.)* If any student or teacher is absolutely certain that this school is on fire, come to my office and tell me, and I'll alert the fire department.

(**BETH** *crosses to the lunchroom as she talks.*)

BETH. *(Confiding to audience.)* A lot of us had been nervous wrecks, wondering when the next alarm was going to go off, so it was nice to finally stop worrying about the Herdmans and get back to our schoolwork.

(Sound effects: School bell.)

(**BETH** *pulls out her Compliments for Classmates journal and joins* **LOUELLA** *in the lunchroom.*)

Scene Five

The Lunchroom – October,
Just Before Halloween

(Lunch tables are decorated with Halloween pumpkins and fall leaves. **BETH** *and* **LOUELLA** *are going over their compliments while nibbling on their sandwiches.)*

LOUELLA. I'm stuck. I've spent a whole month staring at my Compliments for Classmates journal and I've only thought of a few.

BETH. Me too.

LOUELLA. This is much harder than I thought it would be.

BETH. I decided to try doing it in alphabetical order, starting with A.

LOUELLA. A for...Alice? What did you say about Alice?

BETH. *(Reads.)* Alice is important.

LOUELLA. She sure thinks she is.

BETH. Well, she *is* the one the teachers always choose to take notes to the principal's office and the teachers' lounge.

LOUELLA. Yeah, Alice always carries the note with both hands held out in front of her, like it's a message from God.

BETH. And she did always play Mary in the Christmas pageant...until last year.

LOUELLA. Yeah. When the Herdmans took over.

(Starts to write in her notebook.)

Alice...is...important.

BETH. Louella, you can't copy what I wrote. Write your own compliment.

LOUELLA. Okay.

(Erases, reads as she writes.)

Alice is good at carrying important notes to the teachers' lounge.

BETH. I guess that works. But we need a whole page!

LOUELLA. B!

BETH. *(Reads.)* B is for Boomer –

LOUELLA. Who is very cute!

BETH.   – who is good at sports. Especially baseball.

LOUELLA. *(Writes it in her book.)* Boomer is –

BETH. Sporty. A true athlete.

LOUELLA. *(Underlines "very, very" as she speaks.)* – very, very cute!

BETH. *(Whispers.)* Don't write that. Someone might see it and think you like him.

LOUELLA. *(Whispers back.)* I think I do.

BETH. *(Changes subject.)* C is for Claudia.

LOUELLA. I don't know her very well, but she seems nice.

BETH. Her parents are opening the new Soaps 'n' Suds Laundromat next week, so she's probably…

(Writes.) …really clean.

> *(The **HERDMANS** enter in Halloween costumes. **LEROY** is dressed as a pirate with a bandana on his head and an eyepatch. **GLADYS** wears angel wings and a bent halo. **IMOGENE** is in a skeleton mask.)*

GLADYS, LEROY & IMOGENE. Trick or treat!

LOUELLA. Uh oh.

GLADYS & LEROY. Smell my feet.

IMOGENE. Give us something good to eat.

BETH. Halloween isn't until next week.

LEROY, GLADYS & IMOGENE. Not for us!

(**GLADYS** *grabs* **LOUELLA***'s lunch.*)

GLADYS. I'll take that.

LOUELLA. My egg salad!

GLADYS. Egg salad? P-U!

(**GLADYS** *throws it back to* **LOUELLA.***)

BETH. Wow. That really is a Herdman-proof lunch.

LEROY. Come on! Nothin' here.

(**GLADYS** *and* **LEROY** *move on to other* **KIDS.** **IMOGENE** *stays and pushes her skeleton mask up.*)

IMOGENE. Hey, Beth Bradley, lemme look at your journal.

BETH. No, Imogene. That would be cheating.

(**IMOGENE** *grabs* **BETH***'s journal.*)

IMOGENE. I just want to see what you are saying about people.

BETH. Imogene! Give that back!

(*She reaches for the book as* **IMOGENE** *reads.*)

IMOGENE. Ooooh, Boomer is spotty!

BETH. Sporty!

> *(**BETH** grabs back the journal but rips a page
> in the process.)*

IMOGENE. *(Strides off.)* Wait till Boomer hears he's spotty!

BETH. *(Calls after **IMOGENE** angrily.)* Sporty!!

*(To **LOUELLA**.)* Imogene made me tear that page. Now I have to start all over again.

> *(Writes angrily in book, underlining
> adjectives as she speaks.)*

I is for Imogene. Imogene is irritating. And impossible.

LOUELLA. And none of those are compliments.

BETH. Exactly!

> *(**BETH** slams her journal shut.)*

Scene Six
The Bradley Car at the Pick-Up Circle – November

(**MRS. BRADLEY** *is in her car.*)

(*Sound effects: Car horn.*)

[BULLHORN ANNOUNCEMENT]

VOLUNTEER MOM. (*Bullhorn voice-over.*) Keep it moving. No stopping to chat at the Hug-n-Go. We don't want another traffic jam like Halloween. Get in the car and move along.

(*Sound effects: Car engine driving up.*)

(**CHARLIE** *mimes opening rear passenger door.*)

CHARLIE. Mom! Eugene's coming with us.

MRS. BRADLEY. Hi, Eugene. Scoot in.

(**CHARLIE** *and* **EUGENE** *slide onto the bench behind* **MRS. BRADLEY.**)

EUGENE. (*Shyly.*) Hello, Mrs. Bradley.

MRS. BRADLEY. How was school?

EUGENE. (*Mutters.*) Um...fine.

CHARLIE. Eugene and I are doing a fundraiser for the fire department.

MRS. BRADLEY. That's good. They deserve it. Is it just you two?

CHARLIE. No. Everybody. We're all doing fundraising. Here.

(**CHARLIE** *hands her the information flyer.*)

MRS. BRADLEY.   The Kids Care Fundraiser for Fire Fighters. Do-it-yourself?

CHARLIE. Yeah, kids come up with their own fundraising ideas.

MRS. BRADLEY. Every kid?

CHARLIE. Yeah. And the kids who raise the most money by Thanksgiving get a day at –

CHARLIE & EUGENE. Wonderland Amusement Park!

MRS. BRADLEY. Oh, boy!

CHARLIE. With all-you-can-eat pizza.

VOLUNTEER MOM. *(Bullhorn voice-over.)* Keep it moving, Grace!

>(**MRS. BRADLEY** *acknowledges with a wave, then "drives" forward.)*

>*(Sound effects: engine sound, then brakes.)*

CHARLIE. Eugene and I are going to work together.

MRS. BRADLEY. That's great. What are you guys gonna do?

EUGENE. We're not sure yet.

CHARLIE. Everyone is selling lemonade, but Alice Wendleken is selling chocolate chip cookies with hers.

EUGENE. Leroy Herdman wanted to do a cat wash.

MRS. BRADLEY. A car wash. That's a good one.

CHARLIE. No, Mom, a *cat* wash.

MRS. BRADLEY. Cat?

EUGENE. But that didn't work out.

CHARLIE. Leroy took their mangy old cat to the opening of the Soaps 'n' Suds laundromat and tried to stuff it in a washing machine.

EUGENE. That cat shot out of the washer like a rocket.

CHARLIE. He was biting and scratching everyone in sight. People were screaming.

EUGENE. Alice Wendleken's mother called the fire department.

MRS. BRADLEY. That sounds like Mrs. Wendleken.

CHARLIE. Their cat shut down the new laundromat for two whole days.

MRS. BRADLEY. Not a great start for Soaps 'n' Suds.

EUGENE. Now the Herdmans have to come up with a different fundraiser.

CHARLIE. Wonder what it'll be?

EUGENE. Maybe they'll just rob people.

MRS. BRADLEY. I certainly hope not. Say, why don't you boys actually *try* doing a car wash?

CHARLIE. That sounds kinda fun.

EUGENE. I don't think I can. I have a serious reaction to most soaps.

MRS. BRADLEY. How about a dog-walking business? You can start with our dog Hazel.

EUGENE. I'm sorry, Mrs. Bradley, but I'm allergic to dogs.

CHARLIE. Well, we could sell lemonade and instead of cookies, sell chocolate fudge.

EUGENE. I'm sorry but I'm... I'm –

MRS. BRADLEY. – allergic to chocolate?

EUGENE. How did you know?

MRS. BRADLEY. Lucky guess.

> *(Sound effects: Car accelerates out of the Hug-n-Go.)*

Scene Seven
School Hallway

(Sound effects: Kids' voices, lockers slamming or opening.)

(A Ranger Bear cutout wearing a fireman's hat and holding a fire hose is in the hall. Around its neck is a sign reading, "Ranger Bear Really Cares!")

*(As **BETH** speaks, **LOUELLA** lines up next to **BETH** with baby carriage and baby toy, **RALPH** has a rake and stands next to her.)*

BETH. *(To audience.)* For days, all anyone could talk about was what they were going to do for the Kids Really Care fundraiser. Some people, like Alice, got started right away.

*(**ALICE** joins the line-up standing in front of the Ranger Bear cutout, holding a plate of cookies and a pitcher of lemonade, which has a "Ranger Bear wants you to buy my lemonade" sign taped on it.)*

ALICE. Fresh lemonade over here. And chocolate chip cookies that are still warm!

*(**BOOMER** demonstrates raking and **LOUELLA** shakes a rattle in front of the baby stroller as **BETH** talks.)*

BETH. *(To audience.)* Boomer planned on raking leaves for his neighbors. And Louella McClusky asked me to help babysit her brother Howard. Our plan was to keep half the money for ourselves and donate half to the firefighters.

(**ALICE, BOOMER** *and* **LOUELLA** *exit with Ranger Bear, leaving the empty baby stroller on stage.*)

It seemed like a really great plan...until this happened.

(*As scene shifts,* **BETH** *steps to the side to observe.*)

Scene Eight
Downtown Storefront

(On the street in front of a mom-and-pop grocery store. Advertisements for Thanksgiving turkeys are taped to the store window. Next door is the Mane Attraction hair salon.)

*(**LOUELLA** steps out of the store, eating a candy bar, and moves to the stroller.)*

LOUELLA. Howard! I brought you a treat.

(Bends over to offer Howard a bite of her candy bar. He's gone.)

Howard?

(Looks under the stroller.)

Howard!

*(Spins the stroller around and calls for **BETH**.)*

Beth, help! I can't find Howard.

*(**BETH** joins her.)*

BETH. Isn't he in the stroller?

LOUELLA. He was. But even his blankie is gone.

BETH. He couldn't have walked away.

LOUELLA. He can't even crawl yet.

BETH. How did he get out of the stroller?

LOUELLA. I don't know. I just don't know.

(Calls and claps her hands like she's calling a dog.)

Howard! Howard, where are you?

BETH. Louella, even if Howard heard you, he couldn't answer.

LOUELLA. Why not?

BETH. Because Howard can't talk. He's a baby.

LOUELLA. *(Remembering the warnings.)* Stranger danger!

BETH. Now don't get carried away.

LOUELLA. A stranger just walked right up and took my baby brother.

BETH. Then you better tell a policeman.

LOUELLA. Yes – No! He'll tell my mother. And she's not going to be happy about this. We're supposed to watch Howard while she's in the beauty salon.

BETH. Louella, she'll know Howard's missing when she comes out of the salon.

LOUELLA. I've got to find him before she comes out. Who would take my baby brother?

BETH. Someone who doesn't care about his looks.

LOUELLA. What does that mean?

BETH. Howard is bald. Bald as a ping pong ball.

LOUELLA. All babies are bald.

BETH. Not like Howard. His head is bald and shiny.

LOUELLA. That's 'cause my mother rubs Vaseline on it to make his hair grow.

BETH. Ew!

LOUELLA. You're right. Who on earth would want to steal a hairless baby with a greasy head?

      *(**CHARLIE** runs up to join them.)*

CHARLIE. *(Out of breath.)* The Herdmans!

LOUELLA & BETH. The Herdmans?

CHARLIE. The Herdmans have Howard.

LOUELLA. Why?

CHARLIE. They're charging kids twenty-five cents to look at him.

BETH. Who would pay to look at Howard?

CHARLIE. They don't say it's Howard. They have a sign that says, "See the Amazing Tattooed Baby – Twenty-five cents."

LOUELLA & BETH. They tattooed Howard!

CHARLIE. They've already collected $6.50.

LOUELLA. My mother will be so mad. I can't even think how mad she'll be.

BETH. Louella, calm down.

LOUELLA. I can't. This is a disaster. A total disaster!

BETH. Charlie, where are they?

CHARLIE. In the vacant lot by Gleason's Hardware.

> (**CHARLIE** *runs off.*)

BETH. That's close by.

LOUELLA. Come on! We gotta get Howard back.

> *(They start to run just as* **MRS. MCCLUSKY** *steps out of the beauty salon [her hair in foils or in pink perm rollers and a beauty salon cape].* **BETH** *and* **LOUELLA** *try to shield the baby carriage from view when* **MRS. MCCLUSKY** *calls to them.)*

MRS. MCCLUSKY. Louella, it looks like I'll be another hour. Where are you taking Howard?

LOUELLA. Um...to, uh, see, uh...

BETH. To see a tattooed baby.

HAIRDRESSER. *(Voice-over.)* Mrs. McClusky, time to rinse.

MRS. MCCLUSKY. Be right there, Lois.

> *(Turns to go inside, then realizes what* **BETH** *just said.)*

Wait a minute. Tattooed baby! Who on earth would tattoo a baby?

BETH. We're about to find out.

LOUELLA. Bye, Mom!

Scene Nine
Vacant Lot

(The vacant lot.)

(Sound effects: Carnival music from a portable record player.)*

*(**ALICE** and **BOOMER** are watching **LEROY**, sporting a mustache and a plastic checkered tablecloth for a cape, talking through a megaphone [perhaps made of a rolled-up newspaper or cardboard tube]. **IMOGENE** sits on a stool beside him, a cigar box of quarters in her lap. She is wearing a beat-up top hat and has an unlit, half-smoked cigar between her teeth. A bedspread has been draped over a clothesline behind them; pinned to it is a crudely hand-lettered sign that reads: "Tattooed Baby – 25 cents.")*

LEROY. Hur-ry, Hur-ry, Hur-ry! Don't miss your chance to see the Amazing Tattooed Baby.

IMOGENE. You won't believe your eyes.

LEROY. Step right up!

IMOGENE. Just twenty-five cents.

ALICE. A quarter? That's a lot!

BOOMER. You really got a tattooed baby back there?

LEROY. Would I lie to you?

---

* A license to produce *The Best School Year Ever* does not include a performance license for any third-party or copyrighted music. Licensees should create an original composition or use music in the public domain. For further information, please see the Music and Third-Party Materials Use Note on page iii.

ALICE & BOOMER. Yes!

(*Sound effects: Baby cries.*)

BOOMER. That sounded like a real baby.

IMOGENE. Of course, he's real!

LEROY. But don't take our word for it. See for yourself.

IMOGENE. It'll cost you twenty-five cents to find out.

(**BOOMER** *reluctantly pulls quarter from his pocket and hands it to* **IMOGENE.**)

BOOMER. Okay, here.

IMOGENE. (*To* **LEROY.**) He's good to go.

LEROY. (*Ushering* **BOOMER** *behind the curtain.*) You may enter!

BOOMER. (*Laughing.*) Wow! That's incredible!

ALICE. What if I give you one of my yummy chocolate chip cookies?

LEROY. I don't know...

ALICE. It's worth twenty-five cents.

IMOGENE. Make it two cookies.

ALICE. Well...

LEROY. Make it three!

ALICE. Three! That's a lot of cookies.

IMOGENE. No cookies – no tattooed baby.

ALICE. Oh, all right. (*Hands over three cookies.*) There.

LEROY. (*Grandly.*) Enter and be amazed!

(**LEROY** *ushers them behind the blankie.* **ALICE** *screams as* **BOOMER** *laughs in delight.*)

ALICE. Aaaaaah! What happened to him?

BOOMER. He's been tattooed!

ALICE. *(Running off.)* I'm telling!

BOOMER. *(Following* **ALICE.***)* Me too! This is great!

IMOGENE. *(To* **LEROY.***)* Wonderland, here we come!

LEROY. Yes!

> *(Sound effects: Baby cries.)*

> *(***LOUELLA** *and* **BETH** *hurry on with empty baby carriage.)*

LOUELLA. Imogene Herdman! You give me back my baby brother!

IMOGENE. You wanna see the tattooed baby?

> *(Shakes cigar box full of quarters.)*

Twenty-five cents. Fork it over!

LOUELLA. That's no tattooed baby. That's my brother Howard!

LEROY. How do you know?

LOUELLA. Because I just know.

LEROY. You do not.

IMOGENE. It could be anybody's baby.

LEROY. Yeah, it could be somebody's baby you never heard of.

IMOGENE. And it'll cost you a quarter to find out.

LOUELLA. I don't have a quarter.

BETH. I thought your mom gave us a dollar to babysit.

LOUELLA. She did but I may have spent it on a Choco-Whoopee bar.

BETH. Half of that money was supposed to be mine!

LOUELLA. Beth, who cares about that? Now give me back my baby brother!

> (**LOUELLA** *pushes past the* **HERDMANS** *to go behind the bedspread curtain and screams loudly.*)

Howard! What have they done to you!

BETH. Uh-oh.

LOUELLA. Beth! Look what they did to Howard!

> (**LOUELLA** *holds the top of Baby Howard's head up above the bedspread. She speaks from behind the curtain.*)

BETH. That's terrible!

LOUELLA. They drew dogs and cats and...what is that?

BETH. Tic-Tac-Toe.

LOUELLA. They drew a Tic-Tac-Toe on Howard's head!?

BETH. With Magic Markers.

LEROY. *(Holds out a marker to* **BETH.***)* Wanna play?

LOUELLA. No one is gonna play Tic-Tac-Toe on my baby brother's head.

> (**LOUELLA** *lowers Baby Howard's head behind the curtain.*)

BETH. Leroy, you keep that marker away from Howard!

IMOGENE. What are you so upset about?

> (**LOUELLA** *wheels the baby carriage with Baby Howard in it out from behind the bedspread. It faces upstage. All bend over it to look at Baby Howard.*)

LOUELLA. I can't believe this! I just can't!

LEROY. He looks a whole lot better than he did before.

BETH. He does look kind of interesting.

LOUELLA. Interesting?

IMOGENE. Those dogs and cats are a lot better than a big shiny head.

LOUELLA. *(Moans.)* My mother's going to kill me.

BETH. Not if she doesn't know about it. Let's quick take him to my house and wash it off.

> (**BETH** *pushes the baby carriage and pulls* **LOUELLA.***)*

LOUELLA. I am going to die.

BETH. Come on!

IMOGENE. Hey, Louella! Don't forget Howard's blankie.

> (**IMOGENE** *holds the old, dirty, wrinkled and torn blanket out in front of her.)*

BETH. That's really gross.

IMOGENE. Not to Howard.

> (**LOUELLA** *puts the blankie in stroller.)*

LOUELLA. If we ever lost this, Howard would scream and cry and hold his breath till he turned blue.

LEROY. *That* would be worth a dollar!

LOUELLA. And I'd not only be dead, but I'd be grounded for life.

> (**BETH** *and* **LOUELLA** *hurry away; the* **HERDMANS** *call after them.)*

IMOGENE. Scrub his head with Ajax.

LOUELLA. Ajax?

LEROY. And a Brillo pad.

BETH. A Brillo pad?

IMOGENE. It really worked on our cat.

BETH. No wonder that cat is so mean.

LEROY. Don't worry, his hair grew back.

LOUELLA. Come on, Beth, we have to work fast.

> *(The* **GROUP** *exits in different directions as* **BETH** *talks to audience.)*

BETH. *(To audience.)* It turned out it didn't matter how fast we worked. Those Magic Markers were waterproof. So all that scrubbing just turned Howard's head a big smudgy purple. Louella thought if you didn't stand too close and squinted your eyes, the purple kind of looked like veins. But I didn't think so, and neither did Louella's mom. Mrs. McClusky was so mad that she got a sick headache and spots before her eyes and had to lie down for two days. Louella got punished for leaving Howard in front of the grocery store. I was punished for using scouring powder on a baby's head. Even Charlie got punished for giving the Herdmans a quarter just to look at Howard. But nothing happened to the Herdmans. Nothing ever does.

Scene Ten
Mrs. Wendleken's Kitchen/Bradley Kitchen

*(Both **WOMEN** are on the phone, standing in different areas of light.)*

MRS. WENDLEKEN. I tell you, Grace, if anybody but the Herdmans had stolen a baby, and scribbled all over his head, and then charged people to look at him, they would have been grounded for the rest of their natural lives. Where was their mother?

MRS. BRADLEY. Probably at her job. Mrs. Herdman works two shifts at Norton's Shoe factory.

MRS. WENDLEKEN. Two shifts? Where's her husband?

MRS. BRADLEY. I heard he left town and never came back.

MRS. WENDLEKEN. That's just terrible.

MRS. BRADLEY. I don't know how she can possibly keep track of all those kids.

MRS. WENDLEKEN. So tell me, Grace, are Beth and Louella still babysitting Howard?

MRS. BRADLEY. Of course not, Vera. Louella's mother fired them. She said she's not letting Howard out of her sight until he's in college.

MRS. WENDLEKEN. I don't blame her.

MRS. BRADLEY. I'll be glad when this whole "If you care, you have to do-it-yourself" fundraiser for firefighters is over and we can move on to Christmas.

MRS. WENDLEKEN. Christmas! You're not doing the church pageant again, are you?

MRS. BRADLEY. Good heavens, no. Once was enough. But I did get roped into planning the spring talent show.

MRS. WENDLEKEN. Alice will of course be in that. But right now, she's completely focused on winning that fundraiser.

MRS. BRADLEY. You think she will?

MRS. WENDLEKEN. I certainly hope so. Alice is not very good at losing.

MRS. BRADLEY. I heard.

Scene Eleven
The Hallway, With Ranger Bear

(Sound effects: School bell.)

(Sound effects: Hallway noises, kids' voices, lockers slams, etc.)

(BETH, CHARLIE, LOUELLA, *and* **BOOMER,** *gather together clutching books to listen. Ranger Bear is facing upstage.)*

[PA ANNOUNCEMENT]

PRINCIPAL. *(Voice-over.)* Attention, students! May I have your attention, please! It's been a great month of fundraising and the firefighters are very thankful to know how much our kids at Woodrow Wilson really care. And now, I am pleased to announce the winner who raised the most money for our firefighters. It's –

(Muffled sound of hand being put over microphone.)

Mrs. Proctor, are you sure this is correct?

MRS. PROCTOR. *(Voice-over.)* Yes. We counted three times.

PRINCIPAL. *(Voice-over.)* The, uh…Herdman family. The Herdmans have won a trip to Wonderland.

BOOMER, BETH, LOUELLA & CHARLIE. Amazing!/What?/Whoa/No Way!

(Sound effects: A cacophony of mixed response from students.)

(ALICE *runs on, outraged.)*

ALICE. The Herdmans! The Herdmans won? That's just not right. I sold a *lot* of lemonade and cookies!

BOOMER. But the Herdmans really, *really* wanted to win.

ALICE. So did we all. Everyone loves going to Wonderland.

BOOMER. I don't think the Herdmans have ever been.

ALICE. That's just silly. It's right down the road. Their mom could drive them there in fifteen minutes.

BOOMER. Their mom doesn't have a car. She takes the bus. I don't know, maybe it's a good thing that they won.

ALICE. A good thing?

BOOMER. 'Cause now they can go.

(**BOOMER** *turns Ranger Bear around.*)

(*The bear has been vandalized. He wears devil horns instead of a fire hat. A fire hose has been stuck up his nose. Matches and lighters are everywhere on the display and the bear has a cigar butt in its mouth. The* **GROUP** *has different gasps of "Wow! Oh, no!")*

ALICE. *(Aghast.)* Who did that to Ranger Bear?

(*The* **HERDMANS** *run on.* **IMOGENE** *wears the firefighter's hat;* **GLADYS** *is riding piggy-back on* **LEROY.** *They weave in and out of other* **KIDS.***)*

IMOGENE, LEROY & GLADYS. We did it! We won!

IMOGENE. We beat everybody!

LEROY. Number one champeens!

ALICE. *(Marching off.)* I'm telling the principal!

GLADYS. Hooray for us!

(**HERDMANS** *gallop off cheering, while* **BOOMER** *and* **CHARLIE** *exit with Ranger Bear.)*

(**BETH** *steps forward.*)

BETH. *(To audience.)* The Herdmans did get to go to Wonderland despite what Alice told the principal. They even made the newspaper: "Gang of Kids Take Over Amusement Park." And in the end, the roller coaster and Ferris wheel were still standing and the fire department wasn't called. My father thought that being winners might inspire the Herdmans to finally straighten up and fly right. But he was wrong. Leroy proved it!

Scene Twelve
Bradley Car Driving to School Drop Off – December

(Sound effects: Car radio plays holiday music.)*

*(***MRS. BRADLEY*** holds [or mimes] a steering wheel;* **CHARLIE** *sits on a bench beside her as if in the front seat.* **CHARLIE** *holds a glass terrarium on his lap.)*

MRS. BRADLEY. I don't know why you couldn't take your reptile exhibit on the bus, Charlie.

CHARLIE. No pets allowed.

MRS. BRADLEY. But a lizard hardly qualifies as a pet.

CHARLIE. Neither does a spider, but remember last year when Leroy Herdman brought that tarantula on the bus, and it got loose?

MRS. BRADLEY. What a nightmare! Parents had to take turns driving kids to school until the bus driver found that spider.

CHARLIE. After that it was no pets or anything else allowed on bus nine.

MRS. BRADLEY. I don't blame Mr. Gonzales.

CHARLIE. Alice Wendleken still won't get on that bus.

MRS. BRADLEY. Now, keep a tight lid on that terrarium in the classroom. You wouldn't want Leroy Herdman to let your lizard out.

---

* A license to produce *The Best School Year Ever* does not include a performance license for any third-party or copyrighted music. Licensees should create an original composition or use music in the public domain. For further information, please see the Music and Third-Party Materials Use Note on page iii.

CHARLIE. You're right. He's good at that. Hey! That's another compliment for my Compliments for Classmates journal.

(**CHARLIE** *sets the terrarium on the floor in front of him, opens journal and writes.*)

Leroy Herdman is *good* at setting animals free.

(**MRS. BRADLEY** *"stops" the car, mimes putting it in park.*)

MRS. BRADLEY. We're here with five minutes to spare.

(**CHARLIE** *picks up his terrarium, then looks around, a concerned look on his face.*)

CHARLIE. *(Mutters.)* Yeah, um...yeah.

MRS. BRADLEY. Do you need help with the terrarium?

CHARLIE. No, I, uh... I just don't see...um.

MRS. BRADLEY. See what?

CHARLIE. Godzilla, my lizard. He was in here when we left the house.

MRS. BRADLEY. Well, where could Godzilla be?

CHARLIE. Um. Somewhere in this car?

MRS. BRADLEY. You're kidding.

(**MRS. BRADLEY** *yanks her feet up and nervously joins* **CHARLIE** *in looking around the car, between and under the seat. There's a knock on the window. It's Charlie's teacher* **MISS NEWMAN,** *looking pretty frazzled.*)

CHARLIE. *(Whispers.)* Mom, it's my teacher, Miss Newman.

(**CHARLIE** *mimes rolling down the window.*)

MISS NEWMAN. Hi, Charlie. Mrs. Bradley, could...could I sit in your car for a second before school begins?

MRS. BRADLEY. Of course.

MISS NEWMAN. *(Opens the door, scoots in.)* Oh, boy. Oh, boy. Oh, boy.

MRS. BRADLEY. Are you okay?

MISS NEWMAN. I just had a very upsetting experience and I need to take a few breaths before class. And it's so far to the teachers' lounge and I – well, I saw your car out here…

MRS. BRADLEY. What's going on?

MISS NEWMAN. They all warned me not to do my reptile display. Not at *this* school. With *those* kids. But I wouldn't listen. Then this morning when I got here, my classroom door was open.

MRS. BRADLEY. Oh, no. Did someone steal it?

MISS NEWMAN. No, but my baby box turtles were crawling all over the floor.

MRS. BRADLEY. Sounds like Leroy Herdman's handiwork.

CHARLIE. He likes to set things free.

MISS NEWMAN. Then I went to turn on the light in my supply closet. When I pulled the string, it wasn't a string. It was a two-foot-long corn snake.

CHARLIE. That's Ralph's. He loves snakes. And jokes.

MISS NEWMAN. Jokes? It scared the living daylights out of me. And when I ran out of the supply closet, I knocked over the paint pots and now the turtles are covered in red paint. They look like they were attacked.

MRS. BRADLEY. Sounds messy.

> **(EUGENE** *appears outside the car, clutching varying reptiles [rubber snakes, plastic turtles with red paint on their shells, a fake lizard.])*

EUGENE. Miss Newman! Miss Newman! What do I do with these?

MISS NEWMAN. Oh, dear. Now I have to go back inside and see what other reptiles have been let loose.

CHARLIE. Oh, you don't have to go inside, Miss Newman.

MISS NEWMAN. What are you saying, Charlie?

CHARLIE. Godzilla escaped and is somewhere in this car.

MISS NEWMAN. Godzilla!

(Leaps out of the car.)

This is too much!

(Mutters to herself.) Three more days. Only three more days.

MRS. BRADLEY. Miss Newman, what are you talking about?

MISS NEWMAN. Three more days until Winter Break. I just don't know if I can hold on till then.

(Sound effects: Jingle Bells.)*

---

*A license to produce *The Best School Year Ever* does not include a performance license for any third-party or copyrighted recordings. Licensees should create their own.

Scene Thirteen
Outdoor Winter Scene – Winter Break

(Sound effects: holiday instrumental.)*

*(**BETH** and **CHARLIE** are just finishing a snowman with a hat on his head and a carrot nose.)*

BETH. *(To audience.)* You'd think the best thing about winter break would be no Herdmans. But every time it snowed – there they'd be, right outside our door or in the park, blasting everyone with snowballs.

*(Snowballs come from everywhere, hitting **CHARLIE** and **BETH**.)*

HERDMANS. Surprise!

BETH. Take cover!

CHARLIE. Not fair!

HERDMANS. Take that! And that! And that!

BETH. Yeow!

*(**BETH** and **CHARLIE** return fire, hurling snowballs offstage. **LEROY** and **GLADYS** grab the parts of the snowman and run off with them.)*

CHARLIE. They've got Frosty!

BETH. Oh, no you don't!

IMOGENE. Missed me! Missed me!

---

* A license to produce *The Best School Year Ever* does not include a performance license for any third-party or copyrighted recordings. Licensees should create their own.

BETH. *(To audience.)* I tried writing a few compliments about Imogene over the break, but then I thought about her throwing snowballs and ruining my snowman and I got so mad I couldn't write a word.

CHARLIE. Run for it!

(**CHARLIE** *exits.)*

BETH. I was actually looking forward to going back to school!

(**BETH** *crosses to sit on back bench with* **MRS. BRADLEY** *and* **CHARLIE** *on the front bench of the "car.")*

Scene Fifteen
Driving in the Car – January

(**MRS. BRADLEY, CHARLIE** *in front.* **BETH** *in back.*)

(*Sound effects: Car horn.*)

MRS. BRADLEY. Beth, tell Louella we've got to get a move on!

BETH. (*Calling out the car window.*) Louella, hurry!

(*Sound effects: Car horn.*)

We have to go now!

(**LOUELLA** *runs to the car, mimes opening the door.*)

LOUELLA. (*Calls over her shoulder.*) Bye, Mom!

BETH. Get in.

LOUELLA. Sorry, but what's the rush?

MRS. BRADLEY. I want to get to the school early so you kids can post these.

(**MRS. BRADLEY** *passes a handful of flyers to the back seat, hands one to* **CHARLIE.**)

LOUELLA. What are they?

BETH. Sign-up sheets.

BETH, CHARLIE & MRS. BRADLEY. For the spring talent show.

BETH. Night of a Thousand Stars.

MRS. BRADLEY. It's in a month and I'm in charge. Beth, give Louella a pen so she can sign up.

LOUELLA. Wait. I don't have a talent.

MRS. BRADLEY. Yes, you do. Everyone has some talent.

BETH. You're really good at hula-hooping.

CHARLIE. Is that a talent?

MRS. BRADLEY. Of course, it is. Especially if you add music.

LOUELLA. Why should anyone sign up? Alice Wendleken will win.

BETH. She always does.

MRS. BRADLEY. Kids! This year is not a contest. It's a sharing of talents. So everyone wins. And the proceeds all go to the Kids Care Food Drive.

LOUELLA. *(To* **BETH.***)* What are you doing in the show?

BETH. I don't know.

(To audience.) No way was I going to perform, but I couldn't tell Louella that. Mom needed kids to sign up for the show.

(Back to **LOUELLA.***)* I'm still thinking about it.

LOUELLA. *(To* **CHARLIE.***)* How 'bout you, Charlie?

CHARLIE. Me? I'm not going up on that stage!

MRS. BRADLEY. You kids have to do something. It can't just be the Alice Wendleken show.

CHARLIE. Maybe Bernice Potts will do her animal act again this year.

BETH. That wasn't an animal, it was her goldfish.

LOUELLA. Bubbles.

CHARLIE. I thought it was funny.

BETH. *(To audience.)* Bernice stood on the stage asking her goldfish, who was swimming around in that bowl, questions and then told the audience what Bubbles' answers were.

LOUELLA. I don't think Bernice can do it again. Mrs. Wendleken called the principal and said that act didn't belong in a talent show because it didn't have anything to do with human talent.

MRS. BRADLEY. That's ridiculous.

LOUELLA. She said that even if Bubbles could talk, it would be the fish that was talented, not Bernice.

BETH. What about Mary Lou Sampson? She's double-jointed.

CHARLIE. That's right! She can fold herself into a pretzel.

MRS. BRADLEY. Great!

LOUELLA. Yeah, but she needs help unfolding herself.

MRS. BRADLEY. Sounds uncomfortable. Oh, we're here. Grab the flyers.

BETH. Got 'em.

MRS. BRADLEY. And don't forget your lunches and your permission slips for the eye exam.

LOUELLA. Eye exam? That's today?

MRS. BRADLEY. It happens every January. Hold 'em up.

BETH & CHARLIE. Here.

LOUELLA. I forgot mine.

MRS. BRADLEY. Talk to the principal.

(*Sound effects: Whistle blow.*)

VOLUNTEER MOM. (*Bullhorn voice-over.*) Keep it moving, Grace. We've got a lot of kids to unload.

MRS. BRADLEY. Sorry, Nora.

(**KIDS** *jump out of the car.*)

BETH & CHARLIE. Bye, Mom!

LOUELLA. Thanks, Mrs. Bradley.

(They join **KIDS** *walking into the building.* **IMOGENE**, **GLADYS** *and* **LEROY** *huddle nearby.)*

MRS. BRADLEY. *(Calls as she pulls away.)* Make sure everyone sees those sign-up sheets!

IMOGENE. Hey, Beth Bradley. What are we signing up for?

BETH. *(Holds up a sign-up sheet.)* The Night of a Thousand Stars talent show.

GLADYS. Talent show?

IMOGENE. Will there be soda pop and snacks?

BETH. Um, probably.

LEROY, IMOGENE & GLADYS. We're in!

(Sound effects: School bell.)

*(***KIDS** *exit into school.)*

Scene Sixteen
Hall Outside School Nurse's Door

(**KIDS** *stand in line in the hall by the nurse's office.* **ALICE**, **EUGENE** *and* **GLADYS** *are at the head of the line.)*

[PA ANNOUNCEMENT]

PRINCIPAL. *(Voice-over.)* Good morning, students. Today is "We Care About Your Vision Day," brought to you by our local Lion's Club. Be sure to bring your permission slips with you when Mrs. Greenblatt calls your name.

EUGENE. I don't like going to the doctor's office.

ALICE. Mrs. Greenblatt is not a doctor. She's a nurse.

EUGENE. What's she going to do?

GLADYS. Test us.

EUGENE. Tests make me nervous. I'm afraid I'll get a bad grade.

ALICE. This is not that kind of test, Eugene. It's an eye test.

NURSE GREENBLATT. Alice Wendleken.

ALICE. That's me.

NURSE GREENBLATT. Come on in.

(**ALICE** *goes into the exam room.)*

EUGENE. *(Really nervous.)* Oh, no. Oh, no. I don't want to go in there by myself. What's going to happen?

GLADYS. *(Demonstrating.)* You cover up one eye with a piece of cardboard and read the letters on the eye chart. So you'd better know the alphabet.

EUGENE. I know it.

GLADYS. Then you cover up the other eye and read them again.

EUGENE. What if I don't do it right?

GLADYS. That means your eyeballs are in backwards.

EUGENE. My eyeballs are in backwards?

GLADYS. Don't sweat it. They just take your eyeballs out and put them in the other way.

EUGENE. That's terrible. Terrible!

NURSE GREENBLATT. *(Calling out.)* Eugene? Eugene Preston.

GLADYS. That's you.

EUGENE. No, it's not.

GLADYS. Yes, it is.

EUGENE. Is not!

GLADYS. I'll come with you.

> **(EUGENE** *stumbles into the office.* **GLADYS** *follows.* **NURSE GREENBLATT** *hands* **EUGENE** *a black plastic paddle.)*

NURSE GREENBLATT. Cover one eye and read the lowest line on the eye chart with the other eye.

EUGENE. I think that's a B. No, it's an F. I mean, a K. Um, can I step closer?

NURSE GREENBLATT. No.

EUGENE. Please?

NURSE GREENBLATT. Why don't we just switch eyes?

EUGENE. Switch eyeballs? No! No! Nooooooooooooo...

> **(EUGENE** *falls over backwards in a faint.)*

> *(Perhaps* **GLADYS** *catches him.)*

GLADYS. Man down!

NURSE GREENBLATT. Not another.

> *(Scribbles a note and hands it to **GLADYS**.)*

Gladys, take this to Miss Newman in the teachers' lounge right now.

GLADYS. The teachers' lounge! No way! I'm not going near that place. Bad things happen there.

NURSE GREENBLATT. What are you talking about?

GLADYS. Kids go in and they never come out!

NURSE GREENBLATT. That's ridiculous.

GLADYS. That's kidnapping!

NURSE GREENBLATT. Oh, I'll just do it myself. Here. Give Eugene this juice.

> *(**GLADYS** takes the juice box and drinks it down. Then she whaps **EUGENE** on the head with the empty box.)*

GLADYS. Eugene. Wake up.

EUGENE. *(Sits up, groggily.)* My eyeballs.

GLADYS. Eugene. Snap out of it.

EUGENE. Did they switch my eyeballs?

GLADYS. Not yet.

> *(**GLADYS** hands him the empty juice box.)*

EUGENE. Oh, good.

> *(**EUGENE** looks at it and crushes it with his head.)*

GLADYS. Yeow. Did that hurt?

EUGENE. Did what hurt?

(**GLADYS** *whams him with the juice box.*)

GLADYS. That.

(**EUGENE** *just smiles.*)

EUGENE. Naw.

GLADYS. You have a very hard head.

(**EUGENE** *stares at her, not knowing how to respond.*)

(*Smiles knowingly.*) That's a talent.

EUGENE. Thanks.

(**BETH** *enters and talks to the audience. Scene changes behind her.*)

BETH. (*To audience.*) Things happen fast with the Herdmans. By the end of the week, Gladys had become Eugene's manager and entered him in the Night of a Thousand Stars Talent Show, which Mom wanted to change to Night of a Few Stars because only three acts signed up: Mr. McGuffy's kindergarten bellringers, Alice Wendleken, who zipped through "Flying Fingers" on the piano…again. And Eugene Preston, who gave the most amazing performance of all.

Scene Eighteen
Stage for the Night of a Thousand Stars – February

(*Sound effects: Last measures of "Flying Fingers" piano entry.*)

(**ALICE** *walks forward to polite applause, she bows.*)

PRINCIPAL. (*Voice-over.*) Thank you, Alice, for that lovely rendition of "Flying Fingers." As beautifully played as you did at last year's talent show. And the year before. Now –

(**GLADYS** *runs on with microphone she's grabbed from the* **PRINCIPAL.***)*

GLADYS. (*Interrupting.*) Now for some *real* talent. I want you to meet Eugene "Hammerhead" Preston in – The Nutcracker!

(**EUGENE** *enters shyly, carrying a large bowl of walnuts with the word "Nuts!" printed on it. He sits on the stool.*)

(*Calls to sound booth.*) Hit it!

(*Sound effects: Music "Waltz Of The Flowers" from* The Nutcracker Suite.*)

(*As* **GLADYS** *conducts,* **EUGENE** *cracks walnuts against his head in time with the music.*)

---

* A license to produce *The Best School Year Ever* does not include a performance license for any third-party or copyrighted music or recordings. Licensees should create their own.

(*ALICE and* **BETH** *watch from the wings.* **BETH** *says "Ouch!" every time* **EUGENE** *cracks a nut.*)

ALICE. That is not a talent.

BETH. Gladys thinks it is.

(**BOOMER** *runs onstage and leads* **STUDENTS** *in a chant as they count the walnuts* **EUGENE** *cracks.*)

BOOMER. Go, Hammerhead!

BOOMER & STUDENTS (VOICE-OVER). Ham-mer-head! Ham-mer-head! Twenty-eight, twenty-nine, thirty!

(*The music ends, signaling the end of the act.* **LEROY** *and* **GLADYS** *hold up* **EUGENE**'s *arms like a winning boxer.*)

(*Sound effects: Loud applause.*)

PRINCIPAL. (*Voice-over.*) Thank you, Eugene. That was, um, a smashing performance.

GLADYS. We won! We won!!

BOOMER. Hammerhead! You won!

(*Pumps up the crowd, who join him in the chant.*)

Ham-mer-head! Ham-mer-head!

ALICE. (*Trying to shout over the crowd from the wings.*) He did not win. It's not a contest. It's just a show. There is no winner.

(*With a dazed grin,* **EUGENE** *exits, being congratulated by* **GLADYS** *and* **LEROY**.)

GLADYS & LEROY. Way to go, Hammerhead!

(**ALICE** *stomps off as* **BETH** *speaks to the audience.)*

(Sound effects: Nutcracker *music continues under* **BETH***'s speech as the scene shifts.)*

BETH. Eugene became an instant celebrity, with his name in the paper. "Unusual Performance by Plucky Eugene Preston Earns Standing Ovation at School Talent Show." And for the rest of the year, Eugene was no longer Eugene. Even the teachers forgot and called him Hammerhead, just like everyone else.

Scene Nineteen
Outside the Door to the Teachers' Lounge – March

(Sound effects: School bell.)

*(**CHARLIE** is on **BOOMER**'s shoulders outside the door to the teachers' lounge, trying to peer inside through the glass transom. The door is decorated with Easter eggs and bunnies.)*

BOOMER. What do you see, Charlie?

CHARLIE. A sign that says, "Thank God it's Friday!"

BOOMER. What else?

CHARLIE. Another sign that says, "Forty-seven more days till summer."

BOOMER. Just signs?

CHARLIE. No, I see a table…chairs…a coffee maker, and – whoa! Boomer, hold still!

BOOMER. You're getting heavy!

*(**IMOGENE** joins them.)*

IMOGENE. What about beer bottles? Ashtrays? Poker chips?

CHARLIE. No. Why would that be there?

IMOGENE. Because it's the teachers' lounge, where teachers lounge around drinking beer, smoking cigarettes and playing poker.

CHARLIE & BOOMER. What?!

*(**IMOGENE**'s startling news makes **BOOMER** lose his balance; **CHARLIE** jumps off **BOOMER**'s shoulders.)*

IMOGENE. Nobody gets in without a password that changes every week.

BOOMER. How do the teachers know what it is?

IMOGENE. The password is hidden in the morning announcement, like a code. Last week the password was "macaroni-and-cheese."

> (**CHARLIE** *and* **BOOMER** *whisper the password at the door.*)

CHARLIE & BOOMER. Macaroni-and-cheese.

> (*They gingerly push the door. Nothing happens. They try again.*)

Macaroni-and-cheese.

> (*Nothing again.*)

Macaroni-and –

IMOGENE. That was last week's password.

CHARLIE. Then what's this week's?

IMOGENE. I'm not telling.

CHARLIE & BOOMER. *(Disappointed.)* Awwww!

IMOGENE. If a kid goes into that room, they never let him out. Remember Pauline Ellison?

CHARLIE & BOOMER. No.

IMOGENE. Neither does anyone else. Remember Kenneth Weaver?

CHARLIE & BOOMER. Yes.

IMOGENE. Have you seen Kenneth lately?

BOOMER. I heard he had the mumps.

IMOGENE. Kenneth doesn't have the mumps. Kenneth is trapped in the teachers' lounge.

CHARLIE. That's crazy. I don't believe you!

IMOGENE. Neither did Kenneth. I told him he better not go near the teachers' lounge.

(*Shrugs.*)

He did it anyway.

(**IMOGENE** *exits.*)

BOOMER. Do you think Kenneth's really in there?

CHARLIE. No. She just made that whole thing up.

(*Gets out his journal, writes.*)

Imogene is…a…big…liar.

(*He closes the book.*)

Just wait till Kenneth comes back. That'll show her!

(**CHARLIE** *and* **BOOMER** *exit;* **BETH** *appears and looks at the door to the teachers' lounge.*)

BETH. (*To audience.*) But the weeks went on and still no Kenneth. Nobody knew what to believe.

(**LOUELLA** *cautiously joins* **BETH**, *trying to keep* **BETH** *between her and the door.*)

LOUELLA. I don't *think* Imogene Herdman is right and I don't *think* kids disappear into the teachers' lounge, but maybe she *is* and maybe they *do* and I'm not going to take any chances.

(**LOUELLA** *backs away, exiting quickly.*)

BETH. (*To audience.*) I agreed with Louella and stayed as far away from the teachers' lounge as I could.

(*Sound effects: School bell.*)

(**BETH** *hurriedly exits to join Miss Kemp's class.*)

Scene Twenty
Miss Kemp's Classroom – April

(The rolling chalk board reads, "Math Test Today!" The board can also have other reminders, like "How are your Compliments for Classmates coming along?")

MISS KEMP. Math test day!

(Collective groan.)

Don't groan. You know your times tables and you've worked very hard this year. I know you'll ace the test. Now, let's get out our pencils –

*(As **KIDS** get pencils out of their packs or pencil boxes, **IMOGENE** leans over to **BETH**.)*

IMOGENE. Hey, Beth Bradley! Your brother has been telling everyone I'm a big liar.

BETH. Really? Well, it might be considered a compliment. Like something you're really good at.

IMOGENE. *(Suspicious.)* You think?

BETH. Well, yeah.

*(Sound effects: Knock at the classroom door. **MISS KEMP** goes to answer it, sees **CHARLIE**.)*

MISS KEMP. Yes, Charlie. What can I do for you.

CHARLIE. I need to speak to my sister, Beth.

MISS KEMP. We're about to start our math test.

CHARLIE. Please. It's an emergency!

MRS. KEMP. All right but make it quick.

*(To **BETH**.)* Beth, your brother wants to speak to you.

(**BETH** *hurries to the door, they whisper.*)

BETH. What's going on?

CHARLIE. Beth, I was wrong. Kenneth is never coming back. My teacher gathered up his books and moved Bernadette Slocum into his seat. Then she said, "Well, we'll certainly miss Kenneth, won't we?" It's just like Imogene said!

(**BOOMER** *raises his hand.*)

BOOMER. Miss Kemp?

MISS KEMP. Yes, Boomer.

BOOMER. Miss Kemp, I think I need to hear what Charlie is telling Beth. It involves me.

MISS KEMP. What? Why? Well, okay. But make it quick.

(**BOOMER** *joins* **BETH** *and* **CHARLIE** *at the door.*)

BOOMER. Did you say Kenneth is gone. Like gone gone?

CHARLIE. Yes, he's gone gone.

BETH. Oh, come on, Charlie. You know they haven't shut him up in the teachers' lounge.

CHARLIE. I don't know. First, Imogene said Kenneth was *gone* and then he *was* gone. Maybe she's right!

IMOGENE. *(Calls loudly from her seat.)* Of course, I'm right. Kenneth Weaver is toast.

MISS KEMP. What is going on over there? Beth! Boomer! Please return to your seats!

[PA ANNOUNCEMENT]

PRINCIPAL. *(Voice-over.)* Your attention please! Will head custodian Mr. Kaminsky please come to the teachers' lounge? We have an, um, situation. Some kind of trouble with the door lock.

(The **CLASS** *starts whispering. "Teachers' lounge? The lock?")*

BOOMER. Kenneth is trying to break out of the teachers' lounge. And they want the janitor to fix the lock.

CHARLIE. We gotta help him!

*(***BOOMER** *and* **CHARLIE** *bolt out the door.)*

MISS KEMP. Boomer! Come back here. Beth! Sit down.

*(***BETH** *is torn between following them and being a good student and going to her seat.)*

BETH. *(To audience.)* I couldn't let Charlie go to the teachers' lounge by himself. It was too dangerous.

(To **MISS KEMP** *as she exits.)* Sorry, Miss Kemp. I gotta help my brother.

LOUELLA. Me too!

*(***LOUELLA** *runs after* **BETH.** *Meanwhile,* **IMOGENE** *has grabbed a few things from other kids' desks and puts them in her wagon. She heads out the door, too.)*

MISS KEMP. What is going on? Imogene?

IMOGENE. We're setting Kenneth free.

(Exits.)

MISS KEMP. *(Looks at* **ALICE.***)* Well, Alice, it looks like it's just you and me.

ALICE. Does that mean I get an A?

MISS KEMP. Nice try.

[PA ANNOUNCEMENT]

PRINCIPAL. *(Voice-over.)* Mr. Kaminski! Where are you?

Scene Twenty-One
Outside the Door to the Teachers' Lounge

(Sound effects: Loud banging and knocking from inside the teachers' lounge.)

*(***LEROY*** is already at the door as ***BOOMER*** and ***CHARLIE*** arrive. More banging and knocking. ***CHARLIE*** reaches for the doorknob.)*

BOOMER. We're coming, Kenneth!

LEROY. Don't touch that door, Charlie.

CHARLIE. Why?

LEROY. Kids go in and never come out.

CHARLIE. But we gotta save Kenneth!

*(Turns to ***BOOMER***.)* Boomer, you do it!

BOOMER. No way. If Leroy won't do it, I'm not doing it.

*(***BETH*** and ***LOUELLA*** enter.)*

BETH. Is Kenneth all right?

CHARLIE & BOOMER. We don't know.

LEROY. That door is stuck.

(Sound effects: Banging and knocking.)

LOUELLA. What are we going to do?

*(***IMOGENE*** enters, pulling her wagon full of interesting "found" items.)*

IMOGENE. Let me handle it!

LEROY. Imogene, are you sure?

IMOGENE. We gotta save Kenneth.

LOUELLA. *(Murmurs.)* She's brave!

BETH. She sure is!

IMOGENE. That doorknob gets jammed in a locked position.

LOUELLA. We should stay as far away as possible.

BETH. Yeah. Something could blow up or catch fire.

> *(Sound effects: More knocking.)*

LEROY. Hang tight, Kenneth! Imogene's here!

CHARLIE. To save you!

IMOGENE. Boomer! Leroy! Be ready. In case they jump us.

LEROY. *(Assumes a karate pose.)* I'm on it.

BOOMER. *(Imitates* **LEROY.***)* Me too!

IMOGENE. *(To* **CHARLIE.***)* Chuck, I'm going to need your help.

CHARLIE. *(Squeaks.)* My help?

IMOGENE. Yeah.

BETH. Careful, Charlie!

IMOGENE. The rest of you keep a lookout.

> *(***BETH** *and* **LOUELLA** *assume lookout positions.* **IMOGENE** *and* **CHARLIE** *play the next sequence like a surgeon and nurse in the operating room. She holds out her hand to* **CHARLIE,** *requests an item,* **CHARLIE** *repeats the item as he finds it in the wagon and slaps it in* **IMOGENE***'s palm.)*

Squirt gun.

CHARLIE. Squirt gun.

(**IMOGENE** *fires a squirt into the keyhole like she's lubricating the lock. A squeal is heard from inside.*)

MRS. WENDLKEN. *(Muffled voice.)* Yeow!

(**IMOGENE** *passes back the squirt gun, holds out palm.*)

IMOGENE. Measuring thingie.

CHARLIE. Measuring thingie.

(**CHARLIE** *hands her a tape measure.* **IMOGENE** *measures distance to where she's going to pop the door.*)

IMOGENE. Orange Crush.

CHARLIE. Orange Crush.

(Hesitates.) What are you going to do with that?

IMOGENE. Drink it. I'm thirsty.

(**IMOGENE** *guzzles drink as more bangs come from behind the door.*)

MRS. WENDLKEN. *(Muffled voice.)* Let me out!

IMOGENE. Okay. Pink sparkly barrette.

CHARLIE. Pink sparkly barrette.

LOUELLA. My barrette!

(**IMOGENE** *sticks the metal part of the barrette in the lock, pulls the knob towards her.*)

IMOGENE. Now, gimme me the whammer.

CHARLIE. What's a whammer?

BETH. *(Whispers.)* The croquet mallet.

CHARLIE. Oh!! The *whammer.* One whammer coming up.

(**CHARLIE** *hands* **IMOGENE** *the croquet mallet.*)

BOOMER. Wait, that's mine.

IMOGENE. Stand back.

BOOMER. (*Assumes his pose again.*) Right.

LEROY. Kenneth! Be ready to run!

(**IMOGENE** *lines up her shot like a pro golfer.*)

BETH, LOUELLA, BOOMER, LEROY & CHARLIE. (*Counting her swings.*) One...two...three!

(**IMOGENE** *whams the bottom of the door with the mallet and the door flies open.*)

ALL KIDS. Hooray!

(*The* **KIDS** *pat* **IMOGENE** *and* **CHARLIE** *on the back, shouting, "You did it!" "Way to go, Imogene!" "Go, Charlie!"*)

BOOMER. Come on out, Kenneth!

(*To the* **GROUP**'s *astonishment,* **MRS. WENDLEKEN** *stumbles out, looking disheveled. She's holding her cupcake carrier and purse.*)

MRS. WENDLEKEN. Where's that principal?

ALL KIDS. Mrs. Wendleken?!

MRS. WENDLEKEN. I want to talk to Mr. Crabtree right now!

BETH. (*Hisses to* **LOUELLA**.) What's she doing in the teachers' lounge?

LOUELLA. (*Whispers.*) Giving the teachers cupcakes. She does that on test day!

BETH. As a bribe?

LOUELLA. Sounds like it to me.

MRS. WENDLEKEN. *(Shouting.)* Somebody get the principal! And where is my daughter?

BETH. Alice is taking the math test.

BOOMER. Hey! Where's Kenneth?

>(**ALL** *freeze, then walk cautiously towards the half-open door.)*

LEROY. *(Peers inside.)* I don't think he's in there.

MRS. WENDLEKEN. Why would Kenneth be in the teachers' lounge? The Weavers moved to Florida two months ago.

BETH & LOUELLA. Two months ago?

MRS. WENDLEKEN. Before spring break.

>*(A shocked pause. All look at* **IMOGENE**.*)*

IMOGENE. *(Casually mystified.)* Huh.

>*(Sound effects: Bell ring.)*

>*(The* **GROUP** *breaks up going different directions.)*

MRS. WENDLEKEN. *(Calls as she exits.)* Mr. Crabtree!

BETH. *(To audience.)* I was just about to write "Imogene is very brave" in my notebook, but then I realized she isn't brave. She must have known Kenneth wasn't there, which makes it all a big lie. I also realized that finding a single compliment for Imogene might be the hardest thing I'd ever have to do.

Scene Twenty-Two
Recess on the Playground – May

(The **KIDS** *are all out on the playground, jumping rope, playing Four Square with a ball, etc.* **BETH** *sits on bench working on her journal. She is joined by* **LOUELLA** *pushing a baby stroller. Baby Howard is in the stroller, bundled up in a hooded snowsuit with a mittened hand that's visible. His blankie is draped over him.)*

(Sound effects: **KIDS** *chanting a jump rope rhyme: "Not last night but the night before. Twenty-four robbers came knocking at my door.")*

LOUELLA. Beth! Help!

BETH. What do you want me to do?

LOUELLA. Shake this in front of Howard while I unwrap his snack.

BETH. Sure.

*(***LOUELLA** *turns stroller to face upstage and hands* **BETH** *a fun rattle that jingles.* **BETH** *shakes it.)*

Hi, Howie! Hi! I have to say, Louella, I'm really surprised your mom let you babysit Howard again. Hi, little boy!

LOUELLA. Me too. But she was desperate.

*(***ALICE** *joins them.)*

ALICE. My mother says that babies should not be allowed at school.

LOUELLA. It's just for a few weeks, Alice.

ALICE. That's a long time.

LOUELLA. Why do you care?

ALICE. I'm worried about Howard.

LOUELLA. Why?

ALICE. Yesterday at recess, I tried to teach Howard to read, so he'd be ready for kindergarten. But I don't think they'll ever let him into kindergarten. He's pretty dumb.

BETH. He's too little to be dumb.

LOUELLA. If you want to teach him something, teach him to go to the toilet.

        (**ALICE** *covers her mouth in horror.*)

ALICE. *(Hisses.)* Don't say that word.

LOUELLA. Toilet?

ALICE. It's not polite. Mother says you should say ladies' room.

BETH. But Howard is not a lady.

ALICE. Then he can go to the baby boys' room.

LOUELLA. Howard is not going into any rooms. He stays with me. And you know Howard hardly makes a sound.

ALICE. Except when he drops his blankie. Then he won't stop crying.

        (*While* **LOUELLA** *talks, she struggles to pack up the snack;* **BETH** *helps her.*)

LOUELLA. Alice! This is an emergency. My mother had to go out of town to take care of my grandma. And Dad couldn't take Howard to work.

ALICE. Well, my mother says she's going to speak to the principal about it.

LOUELLA. Alice Wendleken, that's just mean!

(Sound effects: School bell.)

BETH. Recess is over! Come on, Louella.

LOUELLA. Yes. Howard and I have to get to class. We have compound fractions to learn.

> *(As **BETH** and **LOUELLA** wheel **BABY HOWARD** off, his blankie drops out of the stroller. **BABY HOWARD** starts crying. **ALICE** gingerly picks up the faded and torn blanket.)*

ALICE. Wait till my mother sees this!

Scene Twenty-Three
Miss Kemp's Classroom – June

(The rolling blackboard has "Compliments for Classmates journals due Monday!!!" written in big bold letters.)

MISS KEMP. Class, before we start today, I have some glad news and sad news. The glad news is that Louella McClusky's father found a babysitter for Howard.

ALICE. *(Smug whisper to **BETH**.)* My mother helped him.

MISS KEMP. The sad news is Howard won't be joining our class anymore this year, but we will always remember him as a big part of our fifth-grade experience.

IMOGENE. Sounds like he died.

MISS KEMP. There is one thing. It seems that Howard went off without his blanket. Has anyone seen Howard's blanket?

IMOGENE. His baby blankie?

LOUELLA. Yeah, it's lost and he's really upset. All he does is cry and hold his breath and hiccup.

ALICE. That blanket is old and full of germs.

*(To **LOUELLA**.)* You should be glad somebody – probably – threw it away. Howard will thank you one day.

IMOGENE. How would *you* know?

MISS KEMP. Now, don't forget, Monday is the day you turn in your Compliments for Classmates journals.

*(General grumbling from the **CLASS**.)*

BOOMER. Monday! That's only a week away!

BETH. A week!

ALICE. I've already finished mine.

BETH. Well, um, I have a few more to go.

(To audience.) That was a fib. I had a lot more to go and I still didn't have one good thing to say about Imogene. Not one!

MISS KEMP. At the end of class on Friday you will each draw a name and read all the compliments you wrote about that one person.

IMOGENE. Out loud?

MISS KEMP. Well, yes.

IMOGENE. Can I go to the bathroom?

MISS KEMP. Now?

IMOGENE. Yes, now. I can't wait.

MISS KEMP. Well, yes, of course, if you can't wait.

> **(IMOGENE** *starts for the door, then turns around and grabs her wagon.)*

IMOGENE. I'm gonna need this.

> **(MISS KEMP** *watches her go out the door, shakes her head.)*

MISS KEMP. I'm not even going to ask.

(Sound effects: School bell.)

Scene Twenty-Four
Hallway Lockers

(All **KIDS,** *except the* **HERDMANS,** *are at their lockers.)*

(Sound effects: Kids' voices, lockers opening and closing.)

BOOMER.   Hey! Someone stole my Compliments for Classmates journal.

BETH. Are you sure you didn't leave it in class?

BOOMER. I'm positive.

*(***BETH*** opens her locker.)*

BETH. Ahhh! Where's *my* journal?

*(***LOUELLA*** checks her locker.)*

LOUELLA. My journal is gone, too!

*(***ALICE*** looks in her locker.)*

ALICE. If this is a joke, I'm not laughing.

BOOMER. *(Runs down the hall.)* Miss Kemp! Miss Kemp! We have a big problem.

(They all run off in one direction uttering about their missing journal. **BETH** *starts to follow, then turns to go the other way.)*

BETH. *(To audience.)* I knew it had to be the Herdmans who stole our journals. But where would they take them? Home? That's a long way from here. They had to be somewhere in our school. And I had to find them before Imogene and Ralph saw what I'd written about them on the pages I was planning to tear out. I had a hunch where they might be.

Scene Twenty-Five
Lunch Room After School

(**IMOGENE**, **LEROY** *and* **GLADYS** *are huddled at a table in the deserted lunch room. They have their journals opened, copying from the pile of gaily-decorated journals spilling out of Imogene's wagon.* **IMOGENE** *is reading out loud and copying from Beth's journal as* **BETH** *enters.*)

IMOGENE. Alice is important. I. M. P. O. R. T. A. N. T.

BETH. Imogene Herdman! That's my journal. You stole it from my locker.

IMOGENE. I didn't steal it. I borrowed it.

BETH. What are you two writing?

LEROY & GLADYS. Nothing.

BETH. You're copying my words.

GLADYS. No, we're not.

(**BETH** *picks up Leroy's journal and reads out loud.*)

BETH. Boomer is spotty.

(*To* **IMOGENE.**) It's *sporty*, Imogene. Boomer is *sporty*.

IMOGENE. (*Shrugs.*) I agree.

GLADYS. (*Reads from her journal.*) Boomer is also very, very cute.

BETH. That's from Louella's journal. That is cheating.

LEROY. Is not.

IMOGENE. We're just borrowing a few words from you.

BETH. And everyone else. That's Bernice Potts' journal, and there's Albert Cooper's and Junior Jacob's.

LEROY. We're gonna put them back as soon as we're done.

BETH. Well, I'm taking mine now and Louella's too.

> (**BETH** *grabs her journal from* **LEROY**, *and reaches for Louella's, which is partially hidden in the wagon under a torn, faded blanket.*)

Wait. That looks like Howard's blankie!

GLADYS. Well, it isn't. That blankie belongs to –

> (**IMOGENE** *cuts in abruptly.*)

IMOGENE. Howard. That blankie is Howard's.

GLADYS. Imogene!

LEROY. *(Whispers under his breath to* **IMOGENE**.*)* What are you doing?

BETH. *You* stole Howard's blankie?

IMOGENE. I would never do that. I found it.

BETH. Where?

> (**IMOGENE** *looks awkwardly at her siblings.*)

IMOGENE. Under...a bush...near the bus stop.

BETH. Under a bush?

IMOGENE. Yeah.

BETH. How did you know it was Howard's?

IMOGENE. Because...of the H written on the corner of the blanket.

> (**IMOGENE** *points to a faded H on the corner of the blanket. [There is also the letter I but it's covered up by the fold.]*)

BETH. H?

IMOGENE. H. For, um, Howard. I was going to put it in Louella's locker.

BETH. Well, give it to me and I'll give it to Louella. Howard will be glad to get this back.

LEROY. *(Grabs the blanket.)* Imogene, no!

(**BETH** *holds out her hand.* **IMOGENE** *gently takes the blankie from* **LEROY**, *holds it to her cheek for a brief second, then thrusts it at* **BETH**.)

IMOGENE. Here. Take it. Don't lose it!

BETH. Imogene, everyone is really upset. You had better put all those journals back where you got them.

IMOGENE. *(Defiantly.)* Maybe I will –

GLADYS & LEROY. And maybe she won't.

BETH. Well... I hope you will.

(**BETH** *walks out of the room, taking a closer look at the blanket as she leaves. She pauses for a second, starts to look back but then decides to go.)*

(**IMOGENE** *picks up another journal and continues copying, wiping at her eye as if she might cry.)*

Scene Twenty-Six
The Bradley House, The Kids' Bedroom

*(Middle of the night. **BETH** is now in her bathrobe. Either she is already in bed or she speaks as she walks to her bedroom, gets in her bed and flicks on a flashlight and stares at her open journal. **CHARLIE** is in the other bed asleep.)*

(Sound effects: Clock chimes two a.m.)

BETH. *(To audience.)* By Sunday night, I had some glad news and sad news of my own. The glad news was the Herdmans had returned all of the Compliments for Classmates Journals. And Howard got his blankie back. But the sad news was I had to read my compliments for one classmate out loud on Monday, and I drew Imogene Herdman's name! I spent the entire weekend trying to think of something good to say about her. And still I had nothing!

*(**MRS. BRADLEY** enters in her bathrobe.)*

MRS. BRADLEY. Beth! Why are you awake? It's the middle of the night!

BETH. Our journals are due tomorrow. I wrote whole pages of compliments for almost everyone in my class, but I drew Imogene's name to read aloud! I don't have one single thing to say about Imogene that counts as a compliment. And this journal is half of my citizenship grade!

MRS. BRADLEY. Read me what you have.

BETH. "Imogene Herdman is very good at stealing other people's belongings. She's also good at cheating and lying."

MRS. BRADLEY. You're right. Those aren't compliments. Can't you think of something nice to say?

BETH. Louella already wrote, "Imogene is healthy." So I can't write that.

MRS. BRADLEY. Didn't you tell me Imogene was the one who let Mrs. Wendleken out of the teachers' lounge?

BETH. Everyone else was too scared to go near the door. I guess that might make Imogene brave. And sort of sneaky, like a burglar, using Louella's pink barrette and Boomer's croquet mallet to unlock the door.

MRS. BRADLEY. She opened the lock with a barrette and a croquet mallet?

CHARLIE. *(Raises head from pillow.)* And me.

*(**BETH** shines the flashlight at **CHARLIE**.)*

BETH. I thought you were asleep.

CHARLIE. I am.

(Flops head back on pillow.)

*(**BETH** shines light at her **MOM**.)*

MRS. BRADLEY. *(Lowers her voice a little.)* I'd call that very resourceful.

BETH. Resourceful?

MRS. BRADLEY. Yes, it means to be able to act imaginatively and effectively in difficult situations.

BETH. Imogene certainly knows how to do that. I think she's got the biggest imagination of anyone I know.

MRS. BRADLEY. Resourceful also means being creative and enterprising.

BETH. Well, she's definitely creative, if you count drawing pictures on baby Howard's bald head. And enterprising, if you count charging money to look at him.

MRS. BRADLEY. See, there's a lot more to Imogene than meets the eye.

BETH. *(Thoughtfully.)* Imogene is also pretty surprising. When Howard lost his blankie and wouldn't stop crying for days and days, Imogene said she found Howard's blanket under a bush and told me to give it to Louella.

MRS. BRADLEY. Under a bush? How did she know it was Howard's?

BETH. It had a faded H written on the corner. She showed me.

MRS. BRADLEY. That's odd.

BETH. What's really odd is it also had the letter I on the blanket.

MRS. BRADLEY. I?

BETH. Yes. I. H. Which I think must be for Imogene. Imogene Herdman. Which means it was *her* blankie.

MRS. BRADLEY. Why do you think Imogene gave Howard her blanket?

BETH. Well, she probably knows how bad Howard must have felt losing his blankie. And I guess she just felt sorry for him.

MRS BRADLEY. So, what does that tell you about Imogene?

BETH. That she's kind? In a weird way.

MRS. BRADLEY. Kind. That's a big one.

(**BETH** *writes "kind" in her journal.*)

It seems like you've got a lot of compliments for Imogene.

(**BETH** *finishes writing and closes the book.*)

BETH. Of course, Alice won't agree with any of them.

MRS. BRADLEY. Well, honey, Alice is just like her mother.

(Quickly.) Don't write that down. And don't tell Alice. That's not a compliment.

(Flashlight off.)

Scene Twenty-Seven
Miss Kemp's Class: Last Day of School

(Sound effects: School bell.)

(The blackboard has compliments written on them describing each student:)

• Alice: important, talented
• Louella: the best big sister, a good friend

BETH. *(To audience.)* The next day, I couldn't believe how nervous I was! We all were. Part of it was having to read compliments about someone out loud and part of it was having to hear compliments about ourselves. When Louella went, Boomer had to sit in a chair in front of her, since she had drawn his name. This made Louella squeal and Boomer's ears turn two or three different shades of red.

LOUELLA. Boomer, you are smart and friendly, and good at sports – but not stuck up about it. I really, really liked when you found Bob, the kindergarten's lost gerbil, dead in your desk after spring break and you took it back to the kindergarten so they could bury it.

MRS KEMP. *(Clapping.)* Thank you, Louella and Boomer. You may now take your seats.

LOUELLA. *(Dreamily to* **BOOMER**, *imagining their wedding.)* I do.

BETH. *(To audience.)* Alice was called next, and she had drawn my name. What could Alice possibly say nice about me, or anybody? I sat in the chair in front of Alice, waiting for the bad news.

*(***BETH*** *sits in the chair, her eyes shut tight.)*

ALICE. Beth Bradley, you are cheerful, a good sport, and fair to everybody. And I know we're not supposed to say things about how people look –

BETH. *(To audience.)* Here it comes.

ALICE. But I've always thought you were graceful –

BETH. What?

ALICE. – because you stand up very straight and you walk like some kind of dancer.

MISS KEMP. Thank you, Alice. That is very observant and very nice.

BETH. *(To audience.)* Alice's words made me feel kind of strange and light. And I thought it was going to be very hard to stand and walk back to my desk, now that I was famous for being so graceful and dancer-like. But I only had to stand because it was now my turn.

MISS KEMP. Imogene?

IMOGENE. What?

MISS KEMP. Let's hear what Beth has to say about you.

IMOGENE. I don't want to.

MISS KEMP. Imogene, you're going to hear good things.

IMOGENE. I'm not so sure about that.

> **(IMOGENE** *covers her ears and squeezes her eyes shut.)*

BETH. Imogene, I wrote that you are brave and kind and resourceful –

IMOGENE. Wait! Wait a minute!

> *(Jumps up, moves to the chair in front of* **BETH.***)*

Start over.

BETH. You are brave, and kind, and very resourceful, which means that you act imaginatively and effectively in difficult situations. You are also inventive. Nobody else thought of taping Donnie Kramer's ears back and buttering his head when he got it stuck in the bike rack. That was very clever of you. And your artistry and creativity, though a little disturbing to baby Howard and his family, is actually what helped you win the Kids Care Fundraiser for Fire Fighters.

MISS KEMP. Thank you, Beth, that is heartfelt and true. And thank you, Imogene.

> (**BETH** *returns to her seat.* **IMOGENE** *stays seated, thinking.*)

Well done, Fifth Grade. You took a good hard look at your classmates and saw that they were more than just outward appearances. I'm so proud of each and every one of you. And since today is the last day of school –

(Sound effects: Fire alarm.)

You have got to be kidding! This is the last day of school!

(Sound effects: Loud cheering from other classes.)

BOOMER. Who pulled the fire alarm?

ALICE. I bet Claude Herdman did it!

> (**MISS KEMP** *tries to get them to line up, but they are all grabbing their belongings and jumping up and down and heading for the door.*)

MISS KEMP. Class! We have to line up. Those are the rules. Class!

> (**IMOGENE** *stops* **BETH**.)

IMOGENE. *(Holds out a magic marker.)* Hey, Beth Bradley, would you write what you said about me on my arm?

BETH. Your arm?

IMOGENE. That's where I keep my notes.

>(**BETH** *looks at* **IMOGENE**'s *arm and reads the messages out loud.*)

BETH. Find cat. Get Gladys. Hmmm. It looks like there's only room for one word.

IMOGENE. Write resourceful. It's the best one. Way better than graceful. No offense.

BETH. Imogene Herdman is –

>(*Writes the word.*)

– resourceful.

IMOGENE. (*Looking at her arm.*) I like it. I'm going to get it tattooed.

>(**IMOGENE** *runs off to join the rest of the kids.*)

BETH. (*To audience.*) It suddenly hit me that Imogene Herdman really was all the things I said she was. And they were good things to be. And then I thought, if Imogene could keep it up until she got to be a responsible adult, she could be almost anything she wanted to be. She could be Imogene Herdman, President. Or, Imogene Herdman, the FBI's Most Wanted. It would be up to her.

>(**CHARLIE** *sticks his head into the classroom.*)

CHARLIE. Beth, come on! Everyone's following Claude Herdman to Johnson's Candy Store.

BETH. Won't we get in trouble?

CHARLIE. Are you kidding? It's the last day of the best school year ever!

(**CHARLIE** *runs gleefully off.*)

BETH. The best school year ever? Really?

(To audience.) The more I thought about it, the more I realized Charlie might be right. I know it was for him. It certainly was for Eugene "Hammerhead" Preston. And the Herdmans, who finally got to go to Wonderland. And Louella, who got to tell the very, very cute Boomer all the things she liked about him. And I think Boomer really liked hearing them. As for me –

IMOGENE. *(Pops head in classroom.)* Hey, Beth Bradley. Free candy! Let's go!

BETH. *(To audience.)* I just might have made a new friend.

(To **IMOGENE.***)* Wait for me!

(**BETH** *joins* **IMOGENE** *and they exit together.*)

End of Play

www.ingramcontent.com/pod-product-compliance
Lightning Source LLC
Chambersburg PA
CBHW070634120726
47909CB00004B/1435